First Words with
Peppa Pig
Level 2

The Best Pet

Based on the Peppa Pig TV series

Peppa Suzy Sheep Zoe Zebra Pedro Pony Doctor Hamster

Learn

are   brown   but   good

he   like   pretty   saw   say

she   this   what   who

toy monkey

tortoise

stick insect

Peppa has a pet fish.

"I like the fish. She is a good fish," said Suzy Sheep.
"She is a pretty fish, Suzy. She is the best pet,"
said Peppa.

Pedro Pony has a pet stick insect.
The stick insect is long and brown.

"What a pretty pet!" said Pedro.
"He is the best pet."

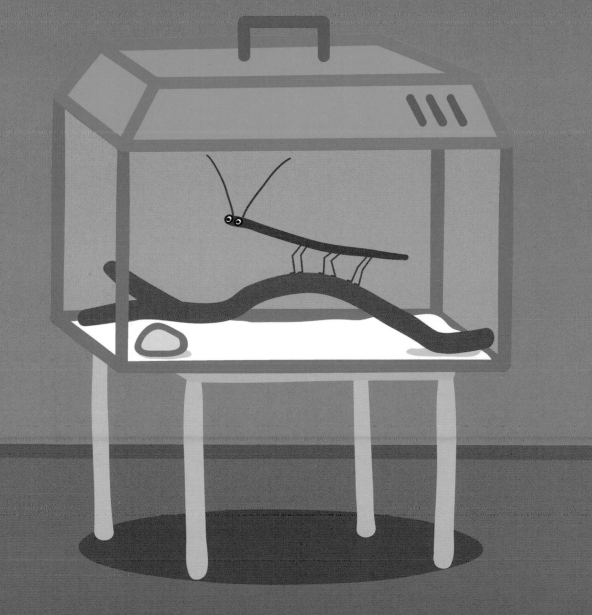

Doctor Hamster will say who the best pets are.

"I like all of the pets! All the pets are pretty," said Doctor Hamster, "But now I will say who the BEST pet is."

Doctor Hamster saw Peppa's pet.
"What is this pet, Peppa?" said Doctor Hamster.
"She is a fish," said Peppa. "Will she win best pet?"

"I like this pretty fish. But I will say who the best pet is soon," said Doctor Hamster.

Doctor Hamster saw Pedro's pet.
"What is this pet, Pedro?" said Doctor Hamster.

"He is a stick insect," said Pedro. "He is long and brown. Will he win best pet?"

"This is a good pet. But I will say who the best pet is soon," said Doctor Hamster.

Doctor Hamster saw Zoe's pet.
"What is this pet, Zoe?" said Doctor Hamster.

"He is a monkey," said Zoe. "He is a brown toy monkey. Will he win best pet?"

"I like this pretty pet. But I will say who the best pet is soon," said Doctor Hamster.

Doctor Hamster saw all of the pets.
"Who is the best pet? I like all of the pets that
I saw, but the best pet is my pet tortoise," said
Doctor Hamster. "And . . ."

"Peppa's fish is the best fish. She is a pretty fish!"
said Doctor Hamster.

"What a good fish!" said Peppa and Suzy.
"We like her!"

"Zoe's monkey is the best brown toy monkey," said Doctor Hamster.
"What a good monkey!" said Zoe. "I like this brown monkey a lot!"

"Pedro's stick insect is the best stick insect.
What a pretty brown pet!" said Doctor Hamster.

"What a good stick insect!" said Pedro. "I like him a lot!"

All of the pets are good pets.
All of the pets are the best pets!